THE CASTLE

Rachel McLean writes thrillers that make your pulse race and your brain tick. Originally a self-publishing sensation, she has sold millions of copies digitally, with massive success in the UK, and a growing reach internationally. She is the author of the Dorset Crime novels and the spin-off McBride & Tanner series and Cumbria Crime series. In 2021, she won the Kindle Storyteller Award with *The Corfe Castle Murders* and her books regularly hit No1 in the Bookstat ebook chart on launch.

Joel Hames is a Lancashire-based writer of crime fiction, and the editor of million-selling books across multiple genres. Joel's own works include the Dead North series featuring lawyer Sam Williams, and the psychological thriller *The Lies I Tell*. Most recently, he has been working with titan of crime fiction Rachel McLean on the hugely successful Cumbria Crime series.

ALSO BY RACHEL MCLEAN AND JOEL HAMES

Cumbria Crime series

The Harbour
The Mine
The Cairn
The Barn
The Lake
The Wood
...and more to come

RACHEL McLEAN & JOEL HAMES

CUMBRIA CRIME NOVELLA

THE CASTLE

Copyright © 2023 by Rachel McLean and Joel Hames

All rights reserved.

No part of this book may be reproduced in any form or by any electronic or mechanical means, including information storage and retrieval systems, without written permission from the author, except for the use of brief quotations in a book review.

This is a work of fiction. Names, characters, businesses, places, events and incidents are either the products of the author's imagination or used in a fictitious manner. Any resemblance to actual persons, living or dead, or actual events is purely coincidental.

Ackroyd Publishing

ackroydpublishing.com

Printed and bound in the UK by CPI Group (Uk) Ltd, Croydon CR0 4YY

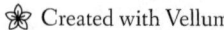 Created with Vellum

CHAPTER ONE

It was going to be a hot morning, Guy thought. But not for a few hours. In the meantime, the only way he was getting any warmth into his body would be by moving it. Fast.

The sun wasn't visible yet, but the sky was beginning to lighten as the ruins of Egremont Castle came into view. The hill rose before him as he peeled off the main road and onto the path. Last week he'd slowed down here, afraid his legs wouldn't take it. When he'd told his daughter, she'd smiled at him: a patient, sympathetic smile that had made him all the more determined to improve. Today, a week fitter, he forced his legs up and down, his breath coming in gasps as he emerged from the trees and took a shortcut across the dew-laden grass to the castle.

Or what had once been a castle. All that was left of the near thousand-year-old building were its walls, and the remains of the gatehouse Guy now ran through.

He felt his heart quicken, the acid building in his legs, the ache beginning to spread.

It was good, that ache. It told him he was working, he was

doing something, getting somewhere. And it had come on later than last week, too. Through the gatehouse as the tip of the sun burst into view over the wall opposite, then three laps of the inner path, anticlockwise this time, the walls towering then dipping beside him. He slowed for the second lap and put on another burst of speed for the final one, then out through the path at the far corner, beside where the Great Hall had once stood.

Downhill now, on uneven ground, his knees jarred. He headed back into the trees and passed a man lying asleep or drunk in the shadows. The man would be cold there, despite it being a hotter-than-usual September. The dew would have soaked into his clothes and chilled his bones.

Guy turned his head as he passed, wondering if he should wake him. How long had he been there? His clothes were wet. Darkness was seeping through his t-shirt.

Guy slowed.

The man wore a white t-shirt. And the darkness that had spread through it – it wasn't entirely black. It wasn't grey, either. It was...

Guy gave a final, disappointed look ahead – this would have been his best run to date – and stopped. He turned and took three steps back towards the ruin.

It's just the sunrise. The sun's rays could add colour to something bland and monochrome. Could even make a white t-shirt look like... like something different. It was just the sunrise.

Except the sun hadn't reached the man yet. He lay on his back in the shadows, motionless, his mouth hanging open. Guy stepped towards him.

Red. The stain on the man's t-shirt was dark red.

"Hello?" he said.

Nothing.

CHAPTER ONE

"Hello?" he repeated, louder, watching for a twitch, for any sign that the man was even breathing.

Still nothing.

Another step closer.

The stain was darker at its centre. Thicker.

Guy bent down and listened at his mouth.

Silence. He watched the chest, trying not to look at the blood. It *was* blood, he couldn't deny it now. Trying to detect any movement at all.

Nothing.

Without taking his eyes off the man, Guy reached into his pocket and pulled out his phone. He glanced down to unlock it and press the numbers, then held it to one ear.

"Hello?" he said. "I think... an ambulance, please. And the police, I think." He stopped. "Please."

Why was he being so polite? So English?

"Yes," he said. "I'm at Egremont Castle. There's a man here with blood all over his chest, and I'm pretty sure he's dead."

CHAPTER TWO

"You could come with me, y'know," whispered DI Carl Whaley. "Just for the day. Get an idea of the place."

DI Zoe Finch opened her eyes and looked up at him. He caught a breath, struck by how beautiful she was between sleep and wakefulness. How lucky he was. There was something almost ethereal about her pale skin and long, red hair.

"Don't be a bloody idiot, Carl," she said, sleep slurring her speech. "Some of us still have criminals to catch."

He grinned. She was less ethereal when she spoke. But ethereal would have been boring.

"Fair enough. I'll call you later."

"Much later." She turned onto her side. It was half past five in the morning; she'd sleep for another hour or two.

He crept out of the room then paused at the top of the stairs. Yoda was staring up at him, her expression radiating outrage at the early hour with the fierce clarity only a cat could communicate. Carl reached down to stroke her and she leapt to the side, grumpy.

CHAPTER TWO

Carl raised his eyebrows – *typical cat* – and straightened up.

The streets were quiet, and he had to concentrate to stay below the speed limit. It wouldn't do to get caught speeding before he'd even started the new job. He waited until he was on the motorway and in the rhythm of the drive before he hit hands-free and told his phone to play voice messages.

There were two. Both from last night. The first was from Maggie in HR, who needed some information about his notice period. He could deal with that tomorrow.

The second was from DCI Branthwaite.

"Hello, Carl? Douglas here." His future boss sounded harassed, even through the heavy Cumbrian accent. "I suppose you're having an early night, what with the drive tomorrow. Look, Carl, on that, there might have to be some changes. Call me, will you? Any time after six tomorrow. I'm an early starter."

Carl glanced at the car's clock. It was past six already. He called Branthwaite.

The DCI answered on the second ring. "Carl. En route, are you?"

"Yes, Sir. Been on the road for half an hour. I just got your message, though. Hope everything's OK?"

"All tickety-boo, Sir. Just some last-minute changes. I'm not going to be in Carlisle today, you see."

"Oh," said Carl.

He'd be starting his new job at Professional Standards – Cumbria Police's anti-corruption unit – in a month. This trip had been planned as a getting-to-know-you sort of outing. Meet Branthwaite, again. Meet his new DS, Denise Gaskill, about whom he knew nothing other than her name and rank. See the station he'd be working in. *But if Branthwaite isn't going to be there...*

"It's OK, Carl." The DCI's booming voice interrupted his thoughts. "Just a change of venue. You've heard about the Hub, haven't you?"

"I have, Sir."

The Cumberland Police Hub was a brand-new purpose-built building a few miles outside Whitehaven. Just a handful of units were stationed there, with more being transferred every week. There was every chance, Carl had been told, that PSD would relocate there eventually, too. Carl wasn't convinced of the wisdom of housing an anti-corruption unit in the same building as the officers they were investigating.

"We'll be there instead," Branthwaite said. "I'll text you the location so you can put it into whatever gizmo you've got guiding you up here. Denise'll be here, too. And it's a decent building. Might even impress a Brummie like you, eh?"

"It might indeed, Sir." Carl didn't point out that he was from Manchester. Birmingham was just where he'd worked for the last three-and-a-bit years.

The Hub, though. He thanked Branthwaite and ended the call. Hadn't he heard something about the Hub?

Wasn't there a DI job up for grabs there?

Zoe was supposed to be looking at jobs herself, applying for anything that wouldn't have them driving a hundred miles in opposite directions once he took up his new role. The Hub would be...

It wouldn't be ideal, not if he started out in Carlisle. But it wouldn't be bad.

He'd have to take a good look at the place.

CHAPTER THREE

Detective Sergeant Aaron Keyes played back the message for the third time as he pushed open the door to the team room. The door was losing its stiffness, finally. It was nice to have a new building to work in, but there were drawbacks.

"I've made a mistake," said a male voice. "I need to speak to you."

There was music in the background, loud, but not so loud Aaron couldn't hear the message. And the caller had given no name, but Aaron knew the voice.

Noah Cane.

DC Nina Kapoor and DC Tom Willis were already at their desks, a good sign. He'd had a word with them both about punctuality when their little team had been put together seven months earlier. And again, last month, after they'd slipped back into their old habits. Things seemed to have improved, and now there they were, ready for work before most of the station was even awake.

It wouldn't hurt to have a DI in place, though. Someone with experience leading a team. Someone to sit between him and Detective Superintendent Fiona Kendrick, absorbing the politics and working out what was an order and what was just a suggestion.

But why had Noah Cane called him?

Cane had left the message just after midnight last night, when Aaron had been fast asleep beside his husband Serge. He'd spotted it at half past six, when he'd woken for the day. He'd played it back over coffee, and wondered what to do about it. He'd toyed with deleting it.

"I've made a mistake. I need to speak to you."

Was it a wrong number? He hadn't come across Cane in... How long? Nearly two years. Cane was a drug dealer, but not an important or successful one. The sort of criminal CID tended to leave alone, unless they got themselves involved in something bigger. The sort of dealer even his customers didn't take seriously. And Cane had sounded drunk, too.

Which was why Aaron had almost deleted the message. Which was why he'd played it back three times and still not returned the call or done anything about it.

"Listen to this," he said.

Tom and Nina, who'd been talking and not noticed him enter, turned to face him.

He played the message.

"Noah Cane?" asked Nina.

Aaron nodded.

She shook her head. "Forget it, Sarge."

"She's right," added Tom. "He won't have anything interesting to say."

Something had caught Aaron's eye. Something on Nina's chair. "What's that?"

Nina arched her back from the chair and twisted her neck

to follow his finger. She grinned. "Mum made it. Crocheted it, then sewed the design on. Like it?"

Aaron didn't want to insult Nina's mother's work. But...

"What is it?" he asked.

"It's an antimacassar."

"A *what*?"

"An antimacassar. You put them on the back of chairs. Stops the chair getting dirty."

Aaron stared at Nina, then at the thing behind her head. "And why's it here?"

Nina grimaced and patted her hair. "She says the quiff isn't... She says the oils leak."

Among her many other talents, Nina was an amateur Elvis Presley impersonator. Aaron had never considered the effort that went into her hair, but it probably involved a lot of product.

He stepped towards her and examined the cover – the *antimacassar* – more closely.

It was mostly white, with holes in it. Deliberate holes, with a certain symmetry. Above the holes was a blank expanse, broken by what Nina had referred to as the 'design'.

"Is that supposed to be a bird?" he asked.

Nina nodded. "A gull. You see that thing in its mouth?"

"Beak," corrected Tom, his voice sounding like he'd been laughing.

Aaron looked at the antimacassar. There was indeed something in the gull's beak. Something that seemed to be grinning at him.

"Er, yes," he replied.

"That," Nina announced, smiling, "is a mackerel."

"It is?" Aaron glanced at Tom, who'd covered his mouth with his hand. *Did the mackerel have gun turrets attached to it?*

Aaron wasn't about to ask. "It's a fascinating object, Nina."

There was a moment of silence, into which Tom's laughter exploded, as if someone had shaken up a bottle of Coke and removed the top.

"Don't worry," Nina said. "I know it's hideous. But Mum made it. She told me it represented Whitehaven, and that I had to bring it to work."

"And if you've met Nina's mum," said Tom, "you'll know to do as she says."

Aaron was trying to come up with a response when Tom's phone rang. The DC answered it, listened, then hung up.

"Stabbing, Sarge," he said. "Egremont Castle."

"Dead?"

"Yup. But that's not all, Sarge. That was Roddy on the phone."

Roddy Chen, the biggest uniformed PC Aaron had ever come across. Intimidating even when he wasn't trying to be, which could be useful.

"Chen spoke?" asked Aaron.

"He's there with the new girl," replied Tom. "Harriet. PC Barnes, Sarge."

Was Tom blushing?

"And?" prompted Aaron.

"And Roddy recognised the body."

"Someone we know, then?"

"You could say that, Sarge. It's Noah Cane."

CHAPTER FOUR

"Connie got that transfer," said Zoe.

Carl thought she sounded flat, but that could have been the signal. There were hills all around them – not hills. Fells.

"Does it make any difference," he asked, "if you're leaving, too?"

"I suppose not." She sighed. "But now she's got it, it all feels a bit more real. Final."

It wasn't just the signal, then. Carl waited.

"I'd hoped to go out with a bang," she continued. "If the team was breaking up. A big collar, something exciting. End on a high."

"I'm sorry," he said. It wasn't easy to sympathise when he was on his way to something that *did* feel exciting.

Another sigh. This wasn't like Zoe, letting things drag her down. Or at least, letting them keep her there.

What she needed was a change of scenery.

Carl caught a shimmer of blue from the corner of his eye, and glanced to his right as a lake came into view. He had no idea which one: so many of them up here. It might just be a reservoir.

It was beautiful. Even on the motorway, the road had woven between the hills, taller and more imposing the further north he got. But here... here was something else entirely.

"You need a change of scenery," he said, then grimaced.

"I've already said I'll come up there with you, haven't I?"

"Yes."

"So you don't need to sell it to me, OK? I'll get myself a job up there and I'll come up and then we'll see if what I need is a change of scenery."

The road turned away from the lake, heading towards one of the fells. Again, Carl had no idea which one it was. Did they all have names?

The sun was behind him, picking out streams and peaks, playing across the folds and chasms carved into the hillside. Dark patches of shade broke up the green.

"Carl?" Zoe said.

Carl had tuned out. "I'm sorry, Zoe. I really—"

"No," she interrupted. "I'm sorry. You're on your way to meet your new team, and here I am putting a downer on everything. Ignore me. I just need another coffee."

"It's OK." He forced his gaze away from the hills and back to the road. "You don't have to be in a good mood all the time. That would be boring."

Zoe laughed.

But it wasn't just a change of scenery she needed.

She'd worked her guts out for West Midlands Police. She'd caught killer after killer, and she'd rooted out so many bad coppers there'd been jokes that Birmingham didn't really need a Professional Standards team. And her reward had been suspicion, the suggestion that some of that corruption must have rubbed off on her. Her DCI had moved to Dorset, replaced by a man who was like a part of the wallpaper by comparison. Her DS had been her closest friend, and he'd buggered off to Scotland. What was left of her team was breaking up.

Zoe was entitled to the odd bad mood. She needed a new team, new colleagues, new challenges. A new life.

But the change of scenery wouldn't hurt.

CHAPTER FIVE

Aaron watched as Stella Berry performed her habitual trick of making coppers feel like they were in her way. Even Nina, who he'd thought would be immune.

As they approached the crime scene, Stella squinted at Nina's quiff, currently being tucked under the hood of Nina's forensic suit. She shook her head, her own peroxide-blonde hair similarly hidden.

"Stella Berry, DC Nina Kapoor," he said.

Nina held out a hand.

Stella looked at it, her hand by her side. She nodded, as if she knew all about Nina, as if she'd summed her up and appraised her in a moment. Nina remained silent.

"Right," Stella said, turning back to her work.

Aaron pulled at the collar of his protective suit, which he'd shrugged on over his actual suit, along with the overshoes covering his black Oxford brogues.

He was sweltering.

Nina had told him not to wear a jacket, and he'd ignored

her. She was dressed in a shirt and skinny black jeans beneath her forensic suit, and didn't seem to be sweating.

Aaron edged closer to her, into a small patch of shade cast by the ruins of what had once been the Great Hall. It barely covered his feet.

Stella was at an advantage. She'd been around dead bodies more times than Nina had sung *Jailhouse Rock*. There were plenty of things Stella might be able to tell them, but not the thing Aaron needed to know.

Could he have prevented this?

If he had called Noah Cane this morning, when he'd first heard the message, would Cane still be alive?

Only one man could answer that, and he wasn't here yet.

"Is this where it happened?" he asked.

Stella nodded. "Blood pattern says yes. No sign of the weapon, though. Probably took it with them."

Aaron followed the trail of blood from the body into the grass and the mass of roots beyond. The man – Noah Cane, even dead, there was no doubt – lay on his back, twisted as if he'd been trying to protect himself, or move away from something. But Aaron knew bodies did their own thing at the moment of death.

The heat was building. By afternoon, it would be sweltering.

"Pathologist ahoy," said Stella.

Aaron looked up to see a man walking up the path towards them, a slighter figure trailing behind him.

"About bloody time," Stella muttered. "This body needs shifting before every fly in England hears about it."

Aaron hadn't met the new pathologist yet. He hoped Dr Robertson would be more helpful than Stella seemed to expect.

The pathologist walked straight up to the body and stared at it for a moment. "Look at this," he said in a local accent Aaron hadn't been expecting. He lifted one of Cane's arms, pressed a gloved finger against it, and watched. Nothing happened. "Non-blanchable. The body's stiff, and starting to go cold already. And then there's the blood. I know it's hot, but it still takes time to dry."

"So what are you saying?" asked Aaron.

The pathologist ignored him. "And look at the damage." He pointed to a mark on the side of Cane's face, just below his ear.

Aaron leaned in, noticing it for the first time. *Was that...?*

"The killer bit him?" he asked.

Dr Robertson gave a short laugh. "I'm sorry. But no. This is the work of the local fauna. Look, obviously I'll have to do a PM, but from what I can see here, I'd say he's been dead for somewhere between five and eight hours. And the cause..." He stood up, looking at Aaron. "Well, it doesn't take a genius, does it?"

"Single stab wound to the heart?" Nina suggested, from behind them.

The pathologist turned. "Clever girl. Cleverer than my lad, at least." He gestured to the young man, watching them from a few steps away then leaned down and examined what he could see of the wound.

"Can't be sure, not yet, but it looks likely. If I had to guess, I'd say it was a sharp, straight-edged blade. Six to ten inches long. I'll know more later."

Aaron and Nina stepped away while Dr Robertson and his 'lad' prepared to move the body.

Somewhere between five and eight hours, the pathologist had said.

CHAPTER FIVE

Noah Cane had been dead long before Aaron had heard his message.

The heat was still there, sweat in the small of his back and running down his face. But the discomfort was gone.

Nina's phone rang. She glanced at Aaron, who nodded. She answered as they walked up into the ruin. The whole area was still cordoned off and would be for the rest of the day.

"It's Tom," she said. Aaron had told him to stay in the office and do some digging into Noah Cane.

"Put it on speaker," Aaron told her.

Tom's voice burst from the phone. "Not a popular man, our Noah Cane. No real friends. The girlfriend, Ella-Rose, she chucked him a few weeks ago and hasn't seen him since, she says."

"We'll have to check on that," Aaron said.

"Got it, Sarge. Shall I ask Uniform to—"

"Not yet. What else have you got?"

"Cane was at the Wheatsheaf last night."

Aaron and Nina had driven right by the Wheatsheaf. They were parked within spitting distance of it. Just a few minutes' walk from where Cane had died.

The prickling sensation was back, but it wasn't heat, and it wasn't discomfort.

Maybe they had something. A piece or two, something to fit in with other pieces. Something that might tell them who had killed Noah Cane.

CHAPTER SIX

Tom heard footsteps and looked up from his screen to see the sarge entering the team room, Nina just behind him. Nina's quiff had collapsed and she scowled as she blew the hair from her face. The sarge was pulling at his shirt, stuck to his body.

Tom pushed back a grin. He'd been left in the air-conditioned office: *short straw*, Nina had said. He wasn't so sure now.

"What have you got?" The sarge draped his jacket over his chair and leaned over Tom's shoulder. A strong floral scent washed over Tom: the sarge had gone heavy on the deodorant.

"Karaoke night at the Wheatsheaf," he said. "I'm going through the CCTV now."

"Did Cane sing?" asked the sarge.

"Manager doesn't think so. And he doesn't remember seeing Cane leave, either. But look. You can see him here."

Tom pointed to a figure in the bottom left corner of the screen. The quality of the image was excellent – in colour, smooth movement rather than jerky leaps. He'd recognised

Cane immediately from the pictures Nina had emailed him from the scene.

The clothes were the same ones the man had been wearing when he died. White t-shirt with a small circular logo on one shoulder; black jeans. And the face, the small, rodent-like features, the swift glance left and right as Cane raised a pint glass to his lips and drained it. Cane was standing at the edge of the open area being used for the singers, his back to the wall. And there was that glance again.

Even if Tom hadn't known who he was, he'd have guessed Cane was used to being watched by the police, or bouncers, or other dealers.

"Is he alone?" asked the sarge.

"He's chatted to people, on and off, but only for a few seconds. I think it's just people he recognises. Quick hello, how you doin', and then off to the next."

"Is he dealing?"

"Not that I've seen. I thought he'd stopped, anyway."

"We haven't heard anything about him, that's true. And unless he grew a new brain in the last few months, he wasn't smart enough to stay off our radar for that long. What's this?"

The sarge pointed at the screen, at Noah Cane stepping away from the wall and moving across the room.

He wasn't alone. There was someone beside him.

"This is what I wanted to show you," Tom said. "It's the last we see of him. He's leaving."

"With this man?"

"Looks like it."

"If it is a man," Nina said.

Tom nodded. *Good point.* He couldn't see the person's face, and there was nothing distinctive about their size or the way they walked.

"Any better views?" asked the DS.

Tom shook his head. "They crop up beforehand, Sarge, but no clearer. I've been through it three times. Whoever it is, they know about the cameras."

The person with Cane was wearing a thin hooded top, the hood up despite the heat. When they turned towards the camera, they ducked or moved their head. Tom couldn't even see their hair.

"What about the cameras outside?" the sarge asked.

Tom shrugged. "All you can see is a bit of arm. If I hadn't known to look for someone else, I'd have thought Cane was on his own. We can ask around, of course. But we might not need to."

"No?" The sarge looked at him.

"Look at this."

Tom took the footage back twenty minutes. Cane was in the corner now, back to the wall. The figure in the hood was talking to him. It was a brief exchange, maybe ten or fifteen seconds. Again, the face was invisible.

But it wasn't Noah Cane or his hooded companion that Tom was pointing at. There were two women behind them, on the makeshift stage, microphones close to their mouths as they sang. Tom was relieved there was no sound on the recording.

"And..." Tom pointed to another woman.

The third woman was laughing. Singing along, pointing at the women on the stage. They pointed back at her in a synchronised, drunken half-dance. But it wasn't the singing or the dancing that had caught Tom's attention.

The woman in front of the stage was holding out her phone, filming her friends.

"I reckon if we can find that woman," he said, "there'll be footage of Cane's companion on her phone."

CHAPTER SIX

"Who is she?" asked Nina.

"No idea. But I've tracked her through the evening. She was there at least an hour. Three drinks, minimum. Look."

He rewound to half an hour earlier. Now the woman stood by the bar with her back to the camera. Her arms were wrapped around someone, their faces close together. They turned, both of them, slightly, and their faces came briefly into view, in profile, lips locked together.

"This isn't your private sex show, Tom," Nina said.

Tom felt his cheeks redden. "You're just jealous."

She chuckled.

"Have you asked the manager who she is?" asked the sarge.

"He's got no idea. Gets busy there, he says. Especially on karaoke night."

The sarge reached forward to stop the footage. "We need to track her down. Get back on with the manager. Find out who else was there, who he knows. We can ask them. If she's local, we're bound to find her eventually."

"Sounds like a pain in the arse, Sarge," said Nina.

"Have you got a better idea?"

"Tom can find her."

"What? How?"

"I don't know," she replied. "He's the computer geek. But I bet you he can do it."

"Can you do it, Tom?" Aaron asked.

Tom considered. He reached forward, changed cameras, and examined the image of the woman filming her friends. Paused it. Stared at it.

It was good. Clear, hardly any movement, no stupid expression on her face. It wasn't perfect. But it would do.

"Yes, Sarge."

"Like hell you can," the DS replied.

"He can, Sarge," Nina said. "Bet you."

A pause.

"OK," said the sarge. "What's the stakes?"

A longer pause. Tom liked it when Nina backed him up like this, even if she was calling him a geek. But what could they—

"I've got it." She pointed to the antimacassar draped over the back of her chair. "Loser keeps that on their chair."

"What, forever?" asked the sarge.

"Until the next bet," Nina told him.

Tom watched as they shook hands. He looked at the antimacassar and shuddered.

Better them than me.

CHAPTER SEVEN

Aaron looked at the back of Nina's chair.

He wanted Tom to find the woman in the CCTV footage, of course. He wanted her, and her phone, and whatever it showed of the person who'd left the Wheatsheaf with Noah Cane.

But he didn't want that *thing* on the back of his chair.

Maybe, if they cracked this quickly, Tom wouldn't get round to finding the woman.

"OK," he said. "We've got some work to do, Nina."

"Sarge?"

"I want a list of Cane's contacts. Not friends; he didn't have any friends. And I know there's no family locally. But the other dealers. Sure, they're rivals, they all hate each other, but they know things about each other. Customers, suppliers, prices, who's got it in for who. Just because Cane dropped off our radar for a while doesn't mean he disappeared. Man like Cane doesn't just get a job in a shoe shop. So we make some calls."

"Got it, Sarge." Nina grabbed her phone.

Aaron turned to Tom, who was still looking at the image of

the woman filming her friends. "Send me that footage, will you?"

"It's in the team inbox," Tom replied.

Aaron sighed. The team inbox, like the team virtual board, was one of the new initiatives that had been imposed with the move to the new building. Aaron thought of himself as being modern, certainly not afraid of technology. But the inbox...

He called up the footage and ran through the scenes again.

There. Just before the woman started filming her friend. Cane, and the figure in the hood. The brief exchange between them. The figure stepped away to reveal the women onstage, behind Cane, microphones to their lips. Aaron winced, even though he couldn't hear a thing.

He watched as Cane pulled his phone from his pocket, walked out of the shot, then returned two minutes later.

Aaron checked the timestamp on the footage, pulled out his own phone, checked when Cane had called him. Seven minutes past midnight.

Shit.

Cane had spoken to this person, this figure in a hood, and he'd called Aaron almost immediately.

"I've made a mistake," he'd said. "I need to speak to you." He'd left half an hour later with that same mysterious figure.

And later that same night, he'd been murdered.

"Sarge." Nina was waving at him. Aaron stood and walked over to her desk. "I've got eight names."

Eight names. Eight dealers. All familiar to Aaron, but he hadn't come across any of them in months.

That was off.

He split the names with Nina, trying to remember if maybe he had seen them, if it had just been something petty, something forgettable, but there was nothing.

CHAPTER SEVEN

He picked one at random. Baz Ingerson. He called, using the contact details on the system: no answer, no voicemail. He tried again using another number, one Baz probably didn't know the police had. A recorded voice told him that the number wasn't recognised.

He tried a second name: Alison Peters. She'd been dealing in Whitehaven for as long as Aaron could remember. Aaron had always had a grudging respect for Alison Peters. She looked like any professional woman on her way to a meeting, and she ran her business like it, too. Cutting customers off if they got too serious or owed too much, not treading too hard on anyone else's feet, living on the wrong side of the law, but so lightly that she could step back again whenever it looked like she might need to.

He had half a dozen numbers for Alison. And now none of them were working.

It had been months since he'd come across her, too. It had been in a bar, in Workington. They'd been looking into a suspicious death. Carly Wheeler. They'd tracked Carly back to the bar, they'd watched the CCTV, they'd found Alison. She'd been straight with them. Yes, Carly had been a customer. Yes, she'd sold to her that night. But that was all.

It had been a suicide, in the end. Not an accidental OD. Not a drug-addled mistake. A suicide. Alison's involvement was a coincidence.

That had been four months ago, and nothing since.

Aaron checked with Nina. She was finding the same thing. She'd been through three and got nothing.

He returned to his desk and called the next one, with the same results. He tried the Police National Computer and was relieved to see that he hadn't imagined all these people. Baz was in HMP Moorland in South Yorkshire, serving three months for drugs offences.

"Same for Topper," Nina said.

"What, same prison?"

"No. Doing a year down south."

Tony Harris, known as Topper on account of his habit of topping up his parcels with a little extra for free, had been someone Aaron had his eye on. He didn't like the way the man did business: cleverly, with an eye to customer satisfaction and long-term loyalty.

But Topper was out of the picture, too. He wasn't the only one.

There were just two left out of the eight. Aaron picked up his phone and called Steve Walker. The phone was answered on the second ring.

"Steve Walker, Mint Condition Motors."

Aaron checked the number he'd dialled. It was right. And it sounded like Steve.

"Steve Walker?" he said.

"Yeah," replied Steve.

It was Steve, wasn't it?

"Steve Walker of Parkfields Road?"

A pause. "Who is this?" asked Steve. "How did you get this number?"

"It's DS Aaron Keyes, Steve. Don't tell me you've forgotten me already."

Another, longer pause. Aaron heard footsteps and a door closing, before Walker spoke again.

"I remember you, DS Keyes. Look, I don't do any of that no more. I don't know who you've been talking to, but I don't have anything to do with drugs these days."

"It's OK, Steve. That's not what—"

CHAPTER SEVEN

"And I'll thank you not to call me when I'm at work." The phone went dead.

Aaron looked up to see Nina looking at him.

"Just got hold of one of them," she said. "Eddie Driver. Remember him?"

Aaron nodded. Driver and Walker had worked together.

"You won't believe this," she said. "He says he's gone straight."

"Don't tell me," Aaron replied. "Selling cars, is he?"

Nina's eyes widened in astonishment.

CHAPTER EIGHT

Aaron hesitated outside the door.

He'd been torn over doing this. He couldn't stand DI Alan Markin – no one could, as far as he knew. Even Markin's own DS, Tracy Giller-Jones, didn't have much time for the man.

Not that Tracy Giller-Jones had much time for anybody.

But Markin was the only DI in the building. There were more coming, eventually. Maybe someone would be recruited to lead Aaron's little team. But in the meantime, it was Superintendent Kendrick or Markin, and there was no way he was going to the super.

"Are you planning on growing roots out there, Sergeant?" came a voice from inside the room.

Aaron grimaced, pushed the door open, and entered.

Markin was in his swivel chair, the top of his stomach showing from the other side of the desk, his head wreathed by sunlight from a window behind him. Aaron squinted as he mumbled a half-greeting, half-apology.

"Sit down, sit down. Still no DI for you?"

"No, Sir." Aaron looked around for somewhere to sit. The

three chairs all had boxes on them, despite Markin being here a month. "Still waiting."

"I'm sure something'll turn up." Markin watched him, looking at the boxes on the chairs. "So what can I do for you, Aaron?"

"It's the local dealers, Sir."

"What about them?"

"They seem to have disappeared. We've been following up on Noah Cane's death, speaking to his associates. Six of them are either in prison or nowhere to be found, and two of them seem to have gone straight." He listed the names.

"Good riddance to bad rubbish." The DI leaned back in his chair.

Aaron frowned. "Well, it's a bit odd, isn't it?"

Markin shrugged. "Odd's one word for it, I suppose. A lucky break might be another."

Aaron sighed. He wasn't going to get any more out of Markin. He headed down to the ground floor to pay a visit to Inspector Keane.

Morris Keane ran most Uniform operations out of the Hub. He wasn't involved in serious crime or intelligence, and had no official interest in things like disappearing dealers. But Inspector Keane, unlike Markin, was someone who prided himself on knowing his patch.

And unlike Markin, Keane had a spare chair in his office. Aaron sat in it, listening to the Inspector complain about one of his PCs, waiting. He told Inspector Keane what he'd found.

"Yes," said Keane, when Aaron had finished.

"Yes?"

"Yes. I'd noticed. Told Markin, as I assume you did. Got the same result you no doubt got."

"No interest."

"No interest," agreed the inspector. "I've asked around a little, or my people have, but there's hardly anyone left to ask, is there? You can't ask the other dealers, because they've disappeared. You can't ask the punters because they're too scared. And you can't ask the suppliers because, well..."

Aaron wondered what Keane wasn't saying. Something about the drugs trade in Cumbria?

Something he didn't want to share, anyway.

"But the upshot is," Keane continued, "we're clueless. Until your Cane turned up this morning, we hadn't heard a peep in weeks. And we're not naïve enough to think everyone round here has suddenly found God and gone clean."

Aaron stood up. "Thanks, anyway."

"I wasn't much help."

Aaron shrugged. He returned to the team room where Nina was making more fruitless calls to even more minor dealers and Tom was staring at his screen.

Was the lack of activity connected to Cane's death? Aaron didn't know. But it was time to pay a visit to some old friends.

CHAPTER NINE

Carl had been waiting no more than a minute in the reception area when DCI Branthwaite strolled in. There was so much building here, so much space, so much metal and glass. Was it meant to impress, or to intimidate? Or was it just money being spent before it ran out?

They shook hands. "Come on then, lad," Branthwaite said, and turned away before remembering the striking dark-haired woman standing beside him. "Oh, yes, this is Denise. She'll be reporting to you, Carl."

"DS Denise Gaskill," said the woman. "Delighted to meet you."

The way she said "delighted" implied the opposite, but Carl shook her hand and said, "Likewise." She had large, dark eyes and looked to be in her early thirties.

DCI Branthwaite, on the other hand, was unremarkable. Sandy hair, average height, glasses. He wore the same grey suit he'd worn at Carl's interview, with a white shirt and blue tie. A different blue tie, slightly paler.

"You coming then, lad?" said Branthwaite, wrinkling his nose.

Carl followed him round a couple of corners and through the custody suite. A handful of uniformed officers lounged by the desk chatting to the custody sergeant, who gave Branthwaite a nod of recognition as they passed. In another corridor, a nervous-looking officer flattened himself against a wall as they marched on. They reached a door, which Branthwaite pushed open.

All this had happened in silence.

"Not really anyone's office, this," Branthwaite explained, "but they let us use it when we need to. They let us do whatever we bloody well want, eh, Denise?"

"It's not as if they have a great deal of choice, Sir," replied the DS.

"So." Branthwaite sat behind the desk, Carl and Denise opposite him. The DCI had leaned forward, staring at Carl. "What do you think then, Carl?"

"It's an impressive building, Sir, but you know that. I'm more interested in the people who'll be working in it. What sort of coppers they are."

Branthwaite smiled. "You see, Denise?" He turned towards the DS. "I told you we had a good one. If you'd heard what this fella got up to in the Midlands... But you won't have, of course. Above your pay grade."

Was Branthwaite rubbing his hands together under the desk?

"I doubt you'll find anything quite so exciting up here," Denise said. "But there should be enough to keep you on your toes, DI Whaley."

A challenge. Wasn't she impressed by her new DI?

Carl shrugged: nothing new.

CHAPTER NINE

They were PSD, after all. Their job was to find bad coppers, and a job like that made a person suspicious, cynical, sometimes even paranoid.

Suspicious and cynical were fine. Good, even. Paranoid could be a problem. Time would tell which side of the line Denise Gaskill fell on.

CHAPTER TEN

Mint Condition Motors was just south of the river, surrounded by showrooms, DIY stores, a supermarket and a sprinkling of fast food outlets. Nina slid into a parking space, spotting a KFC and a McDonald's and closing her eyes while she judged the relative merits of the Big Mac and the Zinger Burger.

"What the hell are you doing?" the sarge asked.

She opened her eyes. "Sorry, Sarge?"

"Do I really have to explain to a serving police officer that she should never close her eyes when she's in control of a moving vehicle?"

Nina shook her head. She might have argued, but she'd already pushed back when the sarge had criticised the state of her car, like it was his business that she had food wrappers all over the back seat.

And if he was in a bad mood now, what would he be like with that antimacassar on the back of his chair? They'd left Tom staring at his screen, focusing on the woman who'd been filming her friends. He'd track her down, Nina was sure.

CHAPTER TEN

As they entered the showroom Eddie Driver hurried towards them, head down, glancing from side to side.

"What the fuck are you doing here?" he hissed when he reached them.

Driver hadn't changed, not since Nina had last seen him, not much since he'd been in school, selling weed by the joint to his fellow year nines while Nina was doing her GCSEs nearly a decade ago. Same mop of thick red-brown hair. Same sense of being uncomfortable in his huge body.

Now he was wearing a suit, a shirt and tie, and shoes that looked almost clean.

"Come for a quick chat, Eddie," she told him. "You didn't want to talk on the phone, you said."

"Fuck's sake." He turned to look around from the corner he'd ushered them into. In the centre of the space, a man with slicked-back hair sat on the reception desk, his legs dangling while he spoke to the bored-looking young woman behind the desk. Neither of them seemed to have noticed Nina and Aaron enter, or Eddie Driver leading them away.

"Steve around?" asked the sarge. "He didn't seem too thrilled to hear from us either."

"Why d'ya reckon that is, DS Keyes?" Eddie glared at them. "What d'you want?"

"Just a chat. Like DC Kapoor said."

"Wait here." Eddie turned and walked away, then stopped and walked back to them. "Don't talk to anyone, right?"

"Whatever you say, Eddie." Nina smiled. He shook his head and hurried away, and she surveyed the room.

She approached one of the cars and ran a hand over it. A Tesla. You saw them all over Cumbria now. Not just being driven by the tourists, but parked in the driveways of locals, outside their offices. How did they afford something like that?

Slicked-back-hair man had noticed her and was ambling over, grinning broadly, looking between her and the car. There was something about the man that made her glad she was about to disappoint him.

She never got the chance. A voice came from behind her.

"We've got this one, Si."

Nina turned to see Eddie, accompanied by a shorter man wearing glasses. Steve Walker.

Wherever Driver was, Walker was never far away. And their names suited them. Driver was sharper, faster. Walker would get there in the end. But sometimes he needed a little help.

"Not sure you can handle a customer of this nature, Eddie." Slicked-back-hair was grinning at her.

"Sorry, love," Nina told him. "They saw me first."

Slicked-back-hair screwed up his nose and walked away. Nina followed Steve and Eddie back to the corner of the room, towards the sarge. The two men muttered between themselves, trying to work out what was going on.

"Come outside." Eddie walked away without waiting, Steve a half-step behind him.

Nina looked at the sarge, who shrugged and nodded. They followed Eddie and Steve into the car park, where Eddie had spotted Nina's car.

"You're still driving that old thing, DS Kapoor?"

"No," she told him. "It's like a stray dog. Just follows me around." She tried not to look at Steve Walker as she said it.

"Very good." Eddie glanced at Steve, then back at Nina. His eyes flashed: *don't talk about my mate like that.*

They'd stopped opposite a handful of nearly-new BMWs and Audis that almost sparkled in the sunlight.

Eddie cocked his head. "If anything catches your eye, let

CHAPTER TEN

me know. I can do you a deal. Anyway, having you lot turn up in the middle of the working day doesn't make us look good. So tell us what you want or clear off, OK?"

"Interesting change of occupation for the two of you," the sarge observed. "What brought you into this line of work?"

"It's sales, isn't it?" Eddie replied. "Don't matter what you're selling. And this way I don't have to worry about knocks on the door in the middle of the night."

"That why you packed in the dealing, is it?" asked Nina. "Knocks on the door?"

"This isn't fair," Eddie said, meeting her gaze. "We got ourselves into trouble a few times, you know that. And if we were still doing all that, then fair enough, come round here and make our lives difficult. But we're not."

Nina glanced at the DS, who nodded.

"So all you're doing here," Eddie continued, "is making life difficult. The boss won't like it if she thinks we're bringing trouble in."

"The boss?" asked Nina.

"Martina," replied Eddie.

"Martina?"

"Martina Mint."

Nina stared at him.

"I don't know what her real name is," he said. "It's what she calls herself, that's all."

"I'm not interested in your boss," interrupted Aaron, "and I'm not interested in screwing up your jobs. Just tell me about Noah Cane."

"Cane? Not seen him for months. He still dealing?"

"No. And he won't be. Noah Cane was found dead this morning. We're trying to speak to people in his line of—"

"I've told you, DS Keyes, we're no longer—"

"I know. And the others?" The sarge reeled off a list of names, the dealers they'd tried to get hold of. Each name was greeted with a shrug.

They might have been lying, of course. But Nina didn't think so.

"So why did you stop dealing?" Nina asked. "Really?"

"I told you," began Eddie

At the exact same moment, Steve said, "Supply-side issues."

"What?" asked Nina.

"Shut up, Steve," said Eddie.

Steve shut up.

CHAPTER ELEVEN

Tom rubbed his eyes and focused again on the image on his screen.

He could see her more clearly now. Late thirties, maybe early forties. Drinking, singing, laughing. From the footage he'd been sent, he couldn't tell when she'd arrived or when she'd left. He couldn't tell if she'd come and gone alone, or with friends, or with the man she'd ended up in a clinch with.

But all that mattered was finding her.

And landing the sarge with that hideous thing Mrs Kapoor had made.

Tom had been through all the footage twice. He'd isolated five moments, each showing the mystery woman from a different angle. He'd taken screengrabs and run them through a piece of AI software that wasn't, as far as he knew, available to the public yet. Software he'd found in a beta version on a forum for global law enforcement tech.

Once he'd given it the images and waited thirty seconds, there she was: a direct headshot, then two side profiles and even a shot from behind.

He compared the image to the ones on the CCTV and nodded.

This was her. Without the effects of bad lighting, rapid movement, or a smudged lens.

He ran the image through a reverse search and sat back to wait as Nina and the sarge walked in.

"Any luck?" asked Nina.

"Nearly," Tom replied. "What about you?"

"Nothing. They don't know about Cane, anyway."

The sarge placed a hand on the back of Tom's chair. "But Steve Walker did say something interesting. We asked him why they'd quit dealing, and he said…" He frowned.

"'Supply-side issues', Sarge," Nina said.

"That was it. Eddie shut him up before he could say any more, but if someone's got control of supply locally and cut out all the old dealers, that might explain what we've seen."

"What, all the disappearances?"

The sarge nodded. "Yup. Going straight, moving away. But I don't see how anyone could take control like that, not without us knowing about it."

Silence.

Tom flicked through the results, his mood brightening as he moved between them. "Got her." He brought up the mystery woman's Facebook profile. "Holly Bowman. Forty-one years old."

"Good work," said the sarge.

"This is yours, I believe." Nina held up the antimacassar and draped it over the sarge's chair. Tom pretended not to notice.

"She's married to… Hang on. Married to Miles Bowman. One daughter, aged eleven. They live in… That's handy."

"What?" asked Nina.

CHAPTER ELEVEN

"They live in Frizington. Just down the road. She works for the water company. And – wait for it... Oh."

"What is it?" asked the sarge.

"She's posted photos from last night. But not the video of her mates singing. The one with Cane and the other one in the background. That one's not here."

"I can get it off her," said Nina. "What's the address?"

The sarge looked at her. "What if she doesn't want to hand it over? This woman's done nothing wrong, and..." He nodded towards the screen, probably thinking what Tom was: that clinch might not be something she wanted to share.

Nina grinned. "I'll talk her round, Sarge."

"You reckon?"

Tom smiled. If anyone could convince a stranger to hand over her video, then it was Nina. "*She* can, Sarge. She'll have it for us by the end of the day."

The sarge looked at the antimacassar. He sighed.

"Care to bet on that, Tom?" he asked.

CHAPTER TWELVE

"While we're here," Branthwaite told Carl, "you might as well meet some people."

"I'd appreciate that," Carl replied.

"You'll be aware that Fiona Kendrick is based here."

Carl had come across Detective Superintendent Kendrick's name while browsing for a new job for Zoe. It was Fiona Kendrick who had a DI vacancy.

"I'd like to meet her," Carl said.

Branthwaite shook his head. "Fiona's busy. But one of the chaps who's usually based in Carlisle is in the building today, and you might as well meet him." He stood up, leaving Carl to follow him out of the office.

"Professional Standards?" asked Carl.

"No," the DCI led him up to a corridor five floors up, doors marked with significant-looking names and titles. He stopped outside a door with no name or title on it and knocked.

"Come in," said a deep male voice.

Branthwaite pushed the door open. "Ralph, this is the man I was telling you about." He turned to Carl. "Denise and I have to be elsewhere, but we'll catch up with you later."

Carl opened his mouth to speak, but Branthwaite was already halfway along the corridor. He shrugged and entered the office.

He held out a hand, having no idea who the man was other than *Ralph*. "Carl Whaley. I'm the new—"

"DI Whaley. I've heard all about you. Ralph Streeting."

Streeting leaned across the desk. Carl tried not to wince as the man's hand closed around his.

Streeting smiled as he squeezed. Unable to reclaim his hand, Carl looked the man up and down. He could be anywhere between his late thirties and early fifties, with faint lines on his face. But the thing that stood out was his suit: it had to be bespoke.

"I'm sorry," Carl told him. "I don't actually know..."

"Typical Doug." Streeting smiled. "DI Ralph Streeting. I'm usually in Carlisle, same as you boys, but like you, my work occasionally takes me a little further afield."

"And that work is?"

Streeting sat down and nodded. "Specialist Crime and Intelligence." His eyes were fixed on Carl's.

"What is that? Organised Crime?"

"Well, Carl." Streeting leaned forward. "It certainly includes that. But it has... Let's just say, it has tentacles."

"Tentacles?" asked Carl.

"My remit extends into a number of areas. But don't worry." Streeting waved dismissively. "If you're straying onto my patch, I'll be sure to let you know."

"That's still not entirely clear," Carl said. "Is there an org chart or something to tell me which areas you're responsible for?"

"Why would you need to know that?"

"I'm PSD, Ralph." Carl returned Streeting's smile. "I need to know everything."

The air stilled. Carl looked into Streeting's eyes. No nameplate, first-name terms with the DCI, 'tentacles'...

After a moment, Carl laughed.

Streeting frowned, then joined in the laugh.

Carl watched him. He'd come across men like Ralph Streeting before. Men who wanted to believe something about themselves: that they were big. Powerful.

Streeting could be the biggest, nastiest dog in Cumbria, as far as Carl was concerned.

As long as he kept his nose clean.

CHAPTER THIRTEEN

Aaron paused outside the door, raised his hand to knock, then let it drop.

Did he really have to do this? Did he have to do it now?

He ran through the day, so far: what they'd learned, what they had yet to learn.

He had to do it now.

He raised his hand again. Maybe she wouldn't be there. She could be in there with someone else. She could be alone. She might not be there at all.

He knocked.

"Come in!"

His heart sank. "Ma'am." He pushed the door open.

Detective Superintendent Fiona Kendrick, Aaron's direct superior for want of a DI or a DCI, was behind her desk. She pointed to the chair opposite and he sank into it as if he'd just run a mile rather than walking up a single flight of stairs.

He always felt diminished in her presence. Diminished and exhausted.

"Aaron. What have you got for me?" She was smiling; she

usually smiled, which made his reaction to her all the more illogical.

"The murder at Egremont Castle, Ma'am. Noah Cane. Thought you might want an update."

"You read my mind, Aaron."

"We're making progress. We've got a rough time of death, he was killed where he was found. We don't have the murder weapon, but it's a single stab wound. We're... We've got a possible lead on someone he was with last night, and we're following up on that. If we can identify them, I think there's a good chance we'll have the killer, Ma'am."

"Excellent." She leaned over the dark wooden desk and picked up a handful of papers.

But he hadn't said what he'd come to say.

"Ma'am. There is something else."

She put down the papers and raised an eyebrow. "Yes?"

He shuffled in his chair. Was he stepping on someone else's toes? Was he seeing something where really there was nothing at all?

"Out with it, Aaron." The super raised an eyebrow. "I know you think you can't waste my time, but it's me or no one, isn't it? If you've got something you're worried about, even if it's nonsense, I'd rather you told me so I can set you straight."

"It's about the dealers, Ma'am." He waited for her to interrupt or prompt. "The local dealers. We were looking into them because—"

"Because Cane was one of them. You don't have to explain the basics. Go on."

He nodded. "Well, they've all disappeared in the last few months. We tried to get hold of eight of them. Four have vanished. Changed their numbers, moved away, no one knows where. Another two are inside, one in Yorkshire, the other down south. But if they hadn't been caught, we wouldn't have known about them, either. And two more have gone straight."

"If you're worried about it, you can ask those two, can't you?"

"We did, Ma'am. They didn't want to talk to us. One of them said something about supply-side issues, but they shut up after that."

"Very well." The Super had interlaced her fingers and was resting her chin on them. "Thank you for bringing this to my attention, Aaron, but it's all in hand."

"In hand, Ma'am?"

"I mean, I'm aware of this... this situation. You can leave it alone. Don't worry about it."

"But, Ma'am—"

She was shaking her head. "You're aware of DI Streeting's Specialist Crime and Intelligence Unit, Aaron?"

"Yes."

"They're handling it. Anything you have to report, you can tell me, or Ralph Streeting. But don't try to pursue this. No one wants you getting your size twelves in the way, Aaron. If your investigation into Cane's murder crosses over into this, well, you may have to hand it over. But I don't think it will. Do you understand?"

He nodded. "Yes, Ma'am."

"Very well." She reached for her papers again.

Aaron stood, thanked her, and left, his mind buzzing as he headed back to the team room.

Something was going on. Something wasn't right.

CHAPTER FOURTEEN

Holly Bowman lived in a clean, whitewashed, semi-detached house – one of the larger ones on Queen's Crescent – a mile from the office. The road gave the impression that the residents cared about how it looked.

Nina parked a few doors down, wiping sweat from her brow as she got out of her car. She noted a red Nissan parked outside the house.

She pressed the bell. Nothing. She knocked.

A moment later the door opened, the chain still on.

"Hello?" said a voice. If this was Holly Bowman, she sounded like she was in pain.

Nina thought back to the images from the night before. The woman had been drunk. She'd gone out with friends, she'd drunk too much, and now she was at home when she was presumably supposed to be at work. Her voice had an ache that Nina reckoned was more than just the booze.

"Mrs Bowman? Are you OK, Madam?"

"Who is it?"

Nina fished for her ID and pushed it through the gap.

CHAPTER FOURTEEN

"Detective Constable Nina Kapoor, Mrs Bowman. I'd like to talk to you about something you might have seen last night, but first I want to make sure you're OK."

The door closed, barely giving Nina time to pull out her hand, and she was left staring at an expanse of red wood. Then it opened. Fully, this time.

Nina saw at once that her instincts had been wrong. Holly Bowman, wrapped in a greying dressing gown, her brown hair falling loose around her shoulders, her face drawn and pale, wasn't in danger. Holly Bowman was hungover.

"You're really the police?" she asked.

Nina nodded. "Can I come in?"

"Yes, yes." The woman ushered her inside, reached around her and pushed the door shut. "Is this... What's this about, then?"

Nina followed her through a hallway, past a prominent family portrait on the wall, and into a kitchen. Holly had already sat down, a cup of coffee on the small round table in front of her.

"Want one?" she asked.

"No, thanks." Nina wouldn't have minded a drink, but she wasn't sure Holly Bowman was in a fit state to make her one. "I wanted to show you this."

She pulled out her phone, navigated to the team inbox, and found the CCTV footage. She put her phone on the table and pressed play.

There was Holly, her phone out, filming her friends. There she was again, singing along with them. There she was, up close and personal with a man beside the bar.

"It's possible," Nina said, "that the footage on your phone, from when you were filming your friends, has something in it that might be of interest to us."

"Interest?" asked Holly.

Nina nodded.

"And I'm not in trouble, right?"

"No, Mrs Bowman. I'd just like to see the footage you took, if that's OK. It would really help us."

"Right," said the woman. "Hang on. Got to find my phone."

She stood, wobbled a little, and wandered out of the room. Nina heard footsteps on the stairs, then above her head. She looked around the room. Three coffee-stained cups sat on the kitchen table. A half-eaten slice of toast on a plate beside the sink.

"Here." Holly stood in the doorway, holding her phone. She presented it to Nina, then pulled it back towards her. "You won't dob me in, right?"

"Don't worry about that," said Nina. She'd rung the woman's workplace, found out she was off sick. "You told them you were ill, didn't you?"

"What?"

Holly sat down, phone in hand, staring across the table at Nina.

It wasn't her unscheduled day off work that she was worrying about, Nina realised. It was what had happened by the bar.

There was a man in the family portrait in the hall. Short, greying, round glasses.

The man Holly had been kissing beside the bar had long, dark hair and was probably a decade younger than her husband.

"Look, it's none of my business," said Nina. "I just want to see your video."

CHAPTER FOURTEEN

Holly stared at her for a moment, then unlocked her phone, tapped open the photos app, and slid it across the table.

There were a dozen videos, and it wasn't until halfway through the fifth that Nina found what she was looking for. As she watched, Holly drifted away, making for the kettle.

"You sure you don't want a coffee?"

"It's OK." Nina looked back down at the phone. There they were, Holly's two friends, microphones right in their faces. Holly had muted the sound before she'd passed Nina the phone. Nina had the sense that the woman had done her a favour.

There was Cane. And there was the figure in the hood. It was a man.

He turned. He was looking at the bar, perhaps, or the exit. He wasn't looking at Holly Bowman's phone, and she wasn't filming him, or not deliberately, at least.

But it didn't matter. Nina could see him, full on, face caught in the overhead light.

And she knew who he was.

CHAPTER FIFTEEN

By the time Nina returned to the office, Aaron had everything ready.

He'd spoken to Inspector Keane, who'd given him two PCs, the same two who'd kept guard over Noah Cane's body. Roddy Chen, who'd be useful if things got nasty, and the new girl, Harriet Barnes. He'd noticed Tom flinch when Harriet's name was mentioned.

The antimacassar, it seemed, was staying on the back of Aaron's chair.

Nina had called him from Holly Bowman's house. She'd forwarded the footage to the team inbox, and there was no doubt about it: the man in the hood was Lucas Wright.

Wright was a nasty piece of work. His record went back to his teenage years, with burglary and affray, which progressed to fixing up stolen cars in his garage, then on to offences involving more violence and more serious weapons as the years passed.

Aaron wouldn't have had Wright down as a murderer, but if it turned out he'd put the knife in Noah Cane, he wouldn't

CHAPTER FIFTEEN

be shocked, either. It was just a few steps up from where Aaron thought he was.

"We go in gentle," he told Nina as he drove. "Like we're just having a chat."

He'd taken his own car this time. It was a short drive to Wright's garage at the north end of Workington, and the time he'd already spent in Nina's car today had been more than enough. The pubs in the centre of town looked busy, long before the end of the working day, drinkers taking advantage of the hot, dry weather before it fizzled out in the usual rain. There would be trouble on the streets tonight.

"But we're not, right?" asked Nina.

Aaron frowned. "Not what?"

"Not just having a chat. Odds are, he killed Cane. We're bringing him in, right?"

"That's right. I just don't want to tip him off."

He pulled up on the pavement a few yards down from Wright's garage. PC Chen parked the squad car behind him. No lights. No sirens. Going in gentle.

He might as well not have bothered.

By the time Nina and Aaron were out of the car, Wright had spotted them.

He stood outside the garage, spanner in one hand, a dark greasy stain on one cheek, staring at them. After a long moment, he turned and ran back into the garage.

Nina didn't wait: she was closer to Wright and ran after him. He paused to open the main door, and that gave her a chance.

He tried to slam the door shut on her, but she caught it with her foot. Aaron, just three steps behind, saw her wince and then push through.

Wright was by a metal door, fiddling with a lock, when Nina caught up with him

She grabbed his arm. He lashed out with the other. She saw it coming and stepped to the side, without releasing his arm.

Instead, she twisted it.

Wright screamed.

Aaron was there a second later, grabbing the loose arm and using his knee to manoeuvre Wright down. By the time Chen walked in, there was nothing left for him to do.

Wright turned and stared at him, then spat.

Aaron recoiled, but was too slow. He was still wiping the man's saliva from his face as he arrested him and read him his rights.

CHAPTER SIXTEEN

Nina had to hand it to Stella Berry, she was quick. She was on the scene muttering something unintelligible before Chen had finished manhandling Lucas Wright into the back of the squad car. By the time they'd pulled away, she'd managed to repeat herself clearly enough for Nina to take offence.

"What did you say?" Nina asked, again.

"I said... For Christ's sake, Huz, get the right fucking box."

Her assistant, a younger man with a short beard and a long, harassed-looking face, scurried back to Stella's car.

"I said," continued the CSM, "you'd better watch out, with that hair. All the electricity in here, sparks and the like. Could go up like a bloody volcano."

Nina stroked her quiff, thinking. *Was it an insult? It was, wasn't it?*

The sarge placed a hand on her shoulder. Nina turned to look at him, to argue, but he was shaking his head, mouthing the words, 'It's not worth it.'

"On second thoughts," added Stella, "if I give you his address, would you pop round to my ex-husband's place? Just slide your hair under the door with a box of matches. Fucking idiot'll manage the rest for himself."

Nina stifled a laugh. If Stella had insulted her, then she wasn't alone. She turned back to say something, but Stella was already at a door at the back of Lucas Wright's garage.

A locked door.

Only, it wasn't locked anymore.

It was a steel door, with one lock embedded in the metal and two padlocks for good measure. Whatever Wright had been keeping in there, he'd wanted it secure.

He hadn't reckoned with Stella Berry.

Nina reached into Tom's backpack and pulled out what she needed, then waited while Stella pushed the door open and looked inside.

It was pitch black in there, but a moment later there was a click, and a bar of light made Nina blink.

She couldn't see anything else from where she was standing, the sarge right behind her. But she could hear the crime scene manager clearly enough.

"Fucking hell," said Stella. "You'll want to take a look at this."

Nina pushed forward, past Stella's assistant, Huz. She stood behind the CSM, mirroring Stella's footsteps as she stepped into the room.

"What the fuck do you think you're doing, Constable?" asked Stella, not turning round.

"What?" asked Nina.

"Contaminating a crime scene. The hair's bad enough at the best of times, but here? You should know better."

"Maybe you should look at the person you're talking to," Nina replied. "Then you might think twice before jumping to conclusions."

CHAPTER SIXTEEN

Stella wheeled round. Nina watched the glare on her face turn to surprise, and then something which was probably the closest the CSM got to shame.

"Where did you get that?" she asked.

Nina pointed behind her to Tom's backpack, permanently stocked with sealed forensic suits, headgear, and shoe covers. Nina had become adept at getting the whole lot on in less than a minute.

"Well," said Stella. "I suppose that's OK, then."

But Nina wasn't looking at her, or listening to her. She was looking at the room in front of her.

It was a small space, more cupboard than room, no more than six feet in each direction. There were shelves on three walls, stacked deep with what Nina was certain weren't car parts.

"How many?" she breathed.

Stella was counting, quietly. "Forty, or thereabouts. Forty fucking handguns in a garage in Whitehaven." The CSM pointed to her left. "And then, of course, there's this."

Nina hadn't noticed the small space to the side, a tiny alcove with its own lighting and another shelf. This one had a single item on it.

A blade, around eight inches long. She looked closer.

"We've got him, Sarge," she breathed. "Bastard hasn't even wiped the blood off."

CHAPTER SEVENTEEN

No hesitation this time, Aaron raised his hand and knocked on the door.

"Come in."

The Super wasn't alone. A man sat opposite her, tall, well-dressed. Familiar.

"Oh," Aaron said.

"Aaron," the super said. "Aaron. You know Ralph Streeting, don't you?"

He nodded. "Ma'am. Sir. I think we've come across each other before."

"Sit." The super gestured towards the only unoccupied chair. "DI Streeting's here on unconnected business, but I've just been updating him on what we discussed earlier."

"What?" Aaron caught himself. "Sorry, Ma'am. What would that be?"

"All the missing drug dealers. Now, what have you got for me? Any news?"

DI Streeting was watching him, eyebrows raised. Aaron was sure he'd seen him before, but couldn't place him.

CHAPTER SEVENTEEN

He'd come to brief the super on the arrest. There was no harm in Streeting hearing about it at the same time.

"We've made an arrest," he said. "For the Cane murder."

"Excellent." She leaned across the desk, beaming. "Anyone we know?"

"Local bad boy. Lucas Wright. He's been in trouble, but this is a step up for him."

"Do you have enough to charge him?" she asked. Streeting looked on, silent.

"We've got the murder weapon. And a confession. He ran as soon as he saw us."

"Motive?"

Aaron glanced at DI Streeting again.

The Super cocked her head. "Would you rather we discussed this in private, Aaron?"

"I..."

"It's OK. Ralph, do you mind stepping away for a bit? I'm sure you have plenty to be getting on with."

DI Streeting stood and smiled at Aaron, then extended a hand. "Good to meet you, Aaron."

A firm handshake, and then they were alone.

"Guns, Ma'am," Aaron said.

"Go on." She leaned forward, hand on her chin.

"Cane had got out of drugs and was helping Wright distribute weapons. Cane decided he wanted out, by the sound of things. Wright couldn't risk him talking. Lured him to the castle and stabbed him."

"And he told you this?"

Aaron nodded. "We have the guns, Ma'am. Around forty handguns in Wright's garage. We need to look into where he got them and who he was planning to pass them on to."

She nodded slowly, frowning. "I take it he won't say?"

"No, Ma'am. He's coughed to the murder. But he won't talk about the guns, other than that he had them and that Cane had decided he didn't want to help him shift them."

The Super sighed and shook her head. "You know what this means?"

"No, Ma'am."

"It means, Aaron, that we're going to have to hand this over to DI Streeting."

Aaron frowned. "This, too, Ma'am? As well as the missing dealers?"

The Super shrugged. "I can't say I'm happy about it. I'd rather we got to follow up our own cases, see them through to the bitter end. But policing's not like that."

Aaron nodded. He could see how this would go. Wright would cut a deal, or try to. Streeting, if he was smart, would convince him there was a deal available.

But there wouldn't be. Lucas Wright had stabbed a man to death in cold blood. He wouldn't be walking away from that before he'd served a life sentence.

"But that's by the by," the super said. "You've done some great work, Aaron. You've solved a murder in less than a day, and that's worthy of congratulations."

She smiled. He forced himself to smile back, remembering what he'd heard about Fiona Kendrick's smile. *The Crocodile.*

"Oh," she added, "I've some news for you."

Aaron stopped himself in the act of standing up, and sat back down. "Yes?"

"We've had an applicant. For the DI job."

"That's good, Ma'am." He hoped it would be.

"It's excellent, Aaron. If she's good enough, you won't have to report directly to me for much longer."

CHAPTER SEVENTEEN

"Who is it, Ma'am?" he asked. "Someone local?"

She shook her head. "She's from Birmingham. She's a DI there. Sparrow, is it?" She looked over at her laptop and tapped on the keyboard. "No. Her name's Finch. Zoe Finch."

CHAPTER EIGHTEEN

CARL HAD a couple of hours to kill before he was due to meet up with DCI Branthwaite again. He left the building and spent some time in Whitehaven, watching the boats in the marina. His meeting with Streeting had left him with a sense of unease, an uncomfortable weight across his shoulders. But now, sitting in the sunshine, watching the mute swans glide in the shallows and chase each other up the slipway, he felt it falling away.

He bought a coffee from a stand and spent a few minutes walking among the grander terraces with their smart blue-and-white painted buildings, and then the side streets with their bars and fast food joints. If they moved here, they wouldn't have to worry about going short of pizzas or kebabs.

On the way back to the Hub, he stopped in a residential area. He'd taken a couple of minutes at the marina to check properties available to rent or buy, and now he spent a few more in his car, idling among the new red-brick houses. Fern Grove, Laurel Court, Holly Bank. There wasn't much sign of ferns or laurels or holly. But you could see the fells in one direction, and as soon as you headed away from the clutch of houses and towards the centre of town, there was the sea.

He shivered. There was something wonderful about it, something exciting.

There was also a man staring at him as he waited for his dog to urinate on the grass verge. Carl smiled at him, and drove away.

Branthwaite was waiting for him in the same room they'd been in before.

"What did you make of DI Streeting?" he asked.

Carl shrugged. "Not sure, Sir." *No point lying.* But he could still be diplomatic about it.

Branthwaite smiled. "Reserving judgment, eh? I can tell you've worked in PSD before, Carl. Now, there's someone I'd like you to meet."

Carl fought back a sigh. Would this be another territorial DI, like Streeting? Or a sarcastic DS who resented the idea of a new boss, like Denise Gaskill? He'd hoped, for one brief, illogical moment, that the police would be somehow better up here. He hadn't really thought about it. It had just seemed possible that the hills and the sea and the clean air would make the coppers cleaner, too.

It was stupid, really. If the coppers were all clean, they wouldn't need PSD. And life would be terribly boring.

"Now," said Branthwaite, "I've had to send Denise back to Carlisle for this. Don't want her meeting this individual. Don't even want her knowing about this individual."

Whatever trepidation Carl had been feeling was replaced by something else.

"What do you mean, Sir? Don't you trust DS Gaskill?"

Branthwaite laughed. "No, it's not that. It's about pay grades. Rank. Look, this Hub, it's all new, of course, but the people working here, they'll be coming from all over, you understand?"

Carl nodded. Branthwaite continued.

"Which means most of them will be clean as a whistle, and some of them won't be. There's a few things we're looking into here."

"Here?" prompted Carl.

"'Here' meaning 'in the Hub'. We don't know who, but we do know there's things happening here that shouldn't be."

"Any examples you can share, Sir?"

"Well, yes. Here's one. We've recently learned that the local drugs scene has dried up."

Carl waited. He knew there were things he could say to fill the silence. Things like *surely that's a good thing*. But it wasn't a good thing. If it was, PSD wouldn't be looking into it.

Branthwaite eyed him. "As you know, drugs scenes don't just disappear. The users still use. The supply still exists, somewhere. If the old dealers have vanished, that just means the new ones aren't on our radar. And that, DI Whaley, is what you'd call suspicious."

"You've got nothing?"

"Well, it's not *us*, as I'm sure you understand. It's not PSD's job to keep track of drug dealers. But yes, the people whose job it is to keep track of drug dealers don't have the faintest idea where they are."

Branthwaite paused, and this time he seemed to be waiting for something.

"Which isn't plausible," Carl said. "Just a few lucky busts in a club would usually be enough to point a half-decent team in the right direction."

CHAPTER EIGHTEEN

"Exactly." Branthwaite nodded. "We've got decent CID here, even if the leadership is a little lacking, but don't tell anyone I said that. And Uniform are second to none. But lately, whenever they find anything, it turns out the drugs came from outside the county. Which, as you say, just isn't plausible. So how come nobody knows anything?"

"Someone knows something," Carl said. "Someone here?"

Branthwaite nodded again. "They're protecting the supply. Which is why we've put someone in play."

"I'm sorry?"

"In play, Carl. We've inserted an officer."

"An undercover operative?"

"Bang on. We've got one right here, Carl. And it's your lucky day."

"How so?"

"DS Gaskill isn't senior enough to meet our operative. But you are."

Carl found himself smiling. He wasn't due to start work here for weeks. But already, he had the sense that it wasn't going to be dull.

Clean coppers were all well and good. But it was the dirty ones that made things interesting.

"Follow me," said Branthwaite. He stood and strode out of the room without waiting for a reply.

Carl followed the DCI back through the custody suite, up two flights of stairs and along yet more corridors until they stopped outside another unmarked door.

"Our operative," Branthwaite announced, pointing to the door. "I'll be waiting downstairs." He turned and walked away.

Carl knocked. Nothing happened.

There was an undercover PSD agent in the room. They'd want to know who was knocking before they invited them in.

"It's DI Carl Whaley," he said. "I'm joining—"

"I know who you are," said a voice. "Come in."

His heart beating loud and fast, Carl pushed open the door and walked inside.

CHAPTER NINETEEN

"I think this calls for a celebration," said Serge.

Aaron was in the car park, on the phone to his husband. He'd called earlier, when they'd first heard about the murder, and told him he'd probably be working late. Serge hadn't been thrilled, but he'd been understanding. He'd known what he was getting into when he'd married a copper, after all. And they'd both known what they were getting into when they'd adopted Annabel.

He'd called back as he headed out of the building to say they'd cracked it, and he'd be home early after all. And someone had applied for the DI job, too. He'd been complaining about having to report to Fiona Kendrick for weeks now.

"A celebration?" he asked.

"Night out. Some food, some drink, a little dancing?"

Serge had put on his fancy French accent – his entirely fake French accent, given he'd been born and raised in Lancaster – and Aaron laughed, despite himself.

"Aren't you forgetting something?" Aaron asked.

"What, our lovely daughter? I'm sure I can find someone to look after her, love."

"I'm not sure," Aaron replied. "I'm just..."

"I know, I know. You don't like the idea of leaving her with a stranger. Fair enough. How about I open a nice bottle of red and cook you something from the finest takeaway Whitehaven has to offer, instead?"

Aaron smiled. "What did I do to deserve you?"

"You're just a winner in life's lottery, DS Keyes. Now, when will you be home?"

Aaron paused, key in the ignition. "There's just someone I need to speak to briefly. I should be home in an hour."

"I can't wait."

He'd been right earlier. Now that the working day was over, the town was packed. He skirted the centre and headed north towards Workington. He parked on a quiet residential street and walked a hundred yards to The Henry Bessemer.

He'd been here before, but not for a while. Walking inside the converted cinema was like stepping into another world, his senses assaulted on all fronts. The place was packed, the bar three deep, music and shouts and laughter echoing around the room, the smell of beer mixed with sweat and the blast of the air conditioning. He stepped away from the door and surveyed the room.

There. Standing near the bar, at the edge of a small group.

Aaron approached, picking his moment, so that the attention of the man's companions was on one of their number, laughing at something he'd said. He walked up to the man and tapped him on the shoulder.

The man turned. He frowned for a moment, then his face cleared in recognition.

CHAPTER NINETEEN

"Victor," said Aaron, trying not to stare at the man's nose ring or his pierced eyebrow. "Buy you a drink?"

CHAPTER TWENTY

Carl had called en route, so Zoe wasn't surprised when she heard the front door open and his voice calling her name.

"In the living room," she called. "I've saved you some pizza."

It had been a long day, dealing with the fallout from the miniature gang war that had erupted in Birmingham, not to mention trying to sort out her own future, and she'd hardly had a chance to eat. She'd planned on waiting for Carl, maybe even going out, but she was too tired and hungry to hang on.

"How was it?" she asked.

He bent over and kissed her on the lips. She could smell something different on him. Something fresh.

Is that all it takes? Drive up the M6 and spend half a day in a new county, and you can become a new person?

"Interesting," he told her. "Met a couple of the team, had a look round the new Hub."

"Oh." Zoe sat up. "I didn't think you'd be based there."

He shook his head, mouth already full of pizza. She waited for him to chew and swallow. He hadn't even sat down yet.

"No," he said as he fell back onto the sofa beside her. "Won't be. But Branthwaite was there, with my new DS, so it made sense to meet them there."

She turned to look at him. He stared at the food, hands poised between a potato wedge and another slice of pizza.

"What did you think of the place?" she asked.

"It's interesting." He bit the end of the potato wedge. "Great building. Not many people in it yet, though. I had time to look around the town, too."

"Whitehaven?"

He turned and gave her the same sort of look she'd been giving him. "Yes," he said. "I thought you didn't know the area."

"I've been doing some research," she said, as he turned on that smile she loved so much. "And that's not all I've been doing."

"Yes?" he asked. There was a slice of pizza in his hand, inches from his mouth, drooping.

"The Hub," she said. "There's a DI job going there."

"I know."

"I applied for it."

The slice fell from his hand.

They both turned to look at it, lying upside-down in a pool of cheese and tomato that spread across his suit trousers in seconds.

Zoe looked back at Carl's face. He was staring at her, eyes wide.

"That's..." she began. "That's OK, isn't it?"

"OK?" he repeated. "OK? It's bloody marvellous."

He picked the slice of pizza up off his leg and turned to her, arms wide. She leaned into them and breathed out.

Later, when they'd finished the food, and Carl had taken

off his trousers and done his best to get rid of the stain, Zoe turned to him again.

"What were they like?" she asked. "The people up there. The coppers."

He shrugged. "OK, I think. I like Branthwaite. He'll take some getting used to, but I think he'll be a good boss. The DS, Denise, she's a bit spiky, but that's probably just her being defensive. I reckon we'll hit it off eventually."

"That's all?" she asked. "You didn't meet anyone else?"

"Not really."

He was staring at the TV, which was switched off.

"Carl?"

He turned to face her. "Yes?"

"You really didn't meet anyone else? In all that time up there?"

He shrugged. "I mean, I spoke to a handful of people. But not for long. Not sure I can even remember their names, to be honest. I didn't meet Fiona Kendrick, if that's what you mean."

"OK." Zoe sat back. It would have been too much of a coincidence. "As long as there isn't anyone who struck you as obviously dodgy, then. I'll probably be working with them all soon, after all."

He laughed.

A forced laugh?

No, she decided, as they made their way up to bed.

She'd imagined it.

Thanks for reading this Zoe Finch story. You can read about Zoe's first case in her new job in *The Harbour*, book 1 of the Cumbria Crime series.

Buy from book retailers or via the Rachel McLean website.

Rachel and Joel

CUMBRIA CRIME BOOK 1, THE HARBOUR

DI Zoe Finch has a lot on her plate.

New job, new team, new county. And on day one, she's plunged straight into a murder investigation.

Zoe has to hit the ground running. She needs to manage a new team with its fair share of challenges, get to grips with a new boss who might not be all she seems, and worry about her reputation following her north to Cumbria.

Can she settle in quickly enough to solve the murder and quell local tensions, as well as coping with an unfamiliar environment?

The Harbour is book 1 in an exciting new series for the star of the bestselling DI Zoe Finch series.

Buy from book retailers or via the Rachel McLean website.

READ THE CUMBRIA CRIME SERIES

The Harbour

The Mine

The Cairn

The Barn

The Lake

The Wood

...and more to come

Buy from book retailers or via the Rachel McLean website.

ALSO BY RACHEL MCLEAN

The DI Zoe Finch Series – buy from book retailers or via the Rachel McLean website.

Deadly Wishes

Deadly Choices

Deadly Desires

Deadly Terror

Deadly Reprisal

Deadly Fallout

Deadly Christmas

Deadly Origins, the FREE Zoe Finch prequel

The Dorset Crime Series – buy from book retailers or via the Rachel McLean website.

The Corfe Castle Murders

The Clifftop Murders

The Island Murders

The Monument Murders

The Millionaire Murders

The Fossil Beach Murders

The Blue Pool Murders

The Lighthouse Murders

The Ghost Village Murders

The Poole Harbour Murders

...and more to come

The Ballard Down Murder, the FREE Dorset Crime prequel

The McBride & Tanner Series – Buy from book retailers or via the Rachel McLean website.

Blood and Money

Death and Poetry

Power and Treachery

Secrets and History

Read the London Cosy Mystery Series by Rachel McLean and Millie Ravensworth – Buy from book retailers or via the Rachel McLean website.

Death at Westminster

Death in the West End

Death at Tower Bridge

Death on the Thames

Death at St Paul's Cathedral

Death at Abbey Road

The Lyme Regis Women's Swimming Club series by Rachel McLean and Millie Ravensworth – buy from book retailers or via the Rachel McLean website.

The Lyme Regis Women's Swimming Club

...and more to come

ALSO BY JOEL HAMES

The Sam Williams Series – Buy now in ebook, paperback and audiobook

Dead North

No One Will Hear

The Cold Years

The Art of Staying Dead

Victims, a Sam Williams novella

Caged, a Sam Williams short

Printed and bound by CPI Group (UK) Ltd, Croydon, CR0 4YY
19/03/2026
02074435-0001